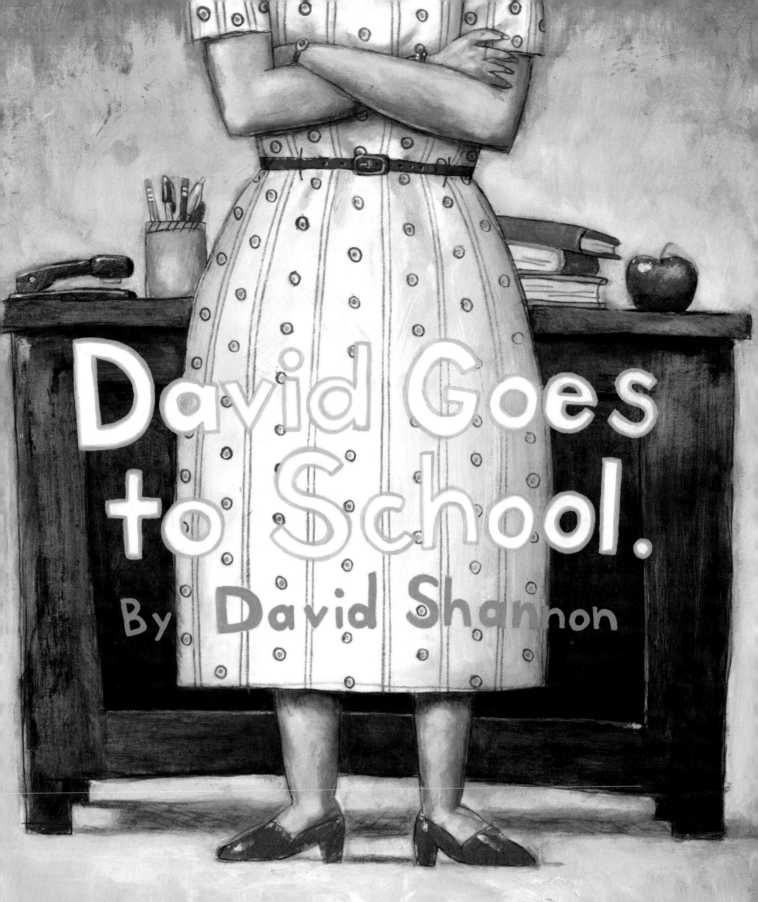

David Goes to School.

By David Shannon

SCHOLASTIC INC.

New York Toronto London Auckland Sydney
Mexico City New Delhi Hong Kong

AUTHOR'S NOTE

A few years ago, my mother sent me a book I made when I was a little boy. The text consisted entirely of the words "no" and "David"—they were the only words I knew how to spell—and it was illustrated with drawings of David doing all sorts of things he wasn't supposed to do. I thought it would be fun to do a remake celebrating all the time-honored ways moms say "no." The new version was called *No, David!*

Well, David's in trouble again. This time it's his teacher saying, "No, David!" It seems that kids haven't changed much over the years, and neither have school rules, some of which date back even farther than the invention of sneakers.

Of course, "yes" is a wonderful word...but "yes" doesn't stop kids from running in the halls.

For Mrs. Harms, Miss Deffert, Mrs. Miller, Mr. Helpingstine,

Mr. Watson, Mrs. Williams, Mr. McDougal, and, of course, Heidi.

This book was originally published in hardcover by the Blue Sky Press in 1999.

ISBN 0-439-22205-2

Copyright © 1999 David Shannon.
All rights reserved.
Published by Scholastic Inc.
SCHOLASTIC and associated logos are trademarks and/or registered trademarks of Scholastic Inc.

12 11 10 9 8 7 6 5 4 3   0 1 2 3 4 5/0

Printed in Mexico   49

First Scholastic paper-over-board printing, September 2000

Keep your hands

Wait your

turn, David!

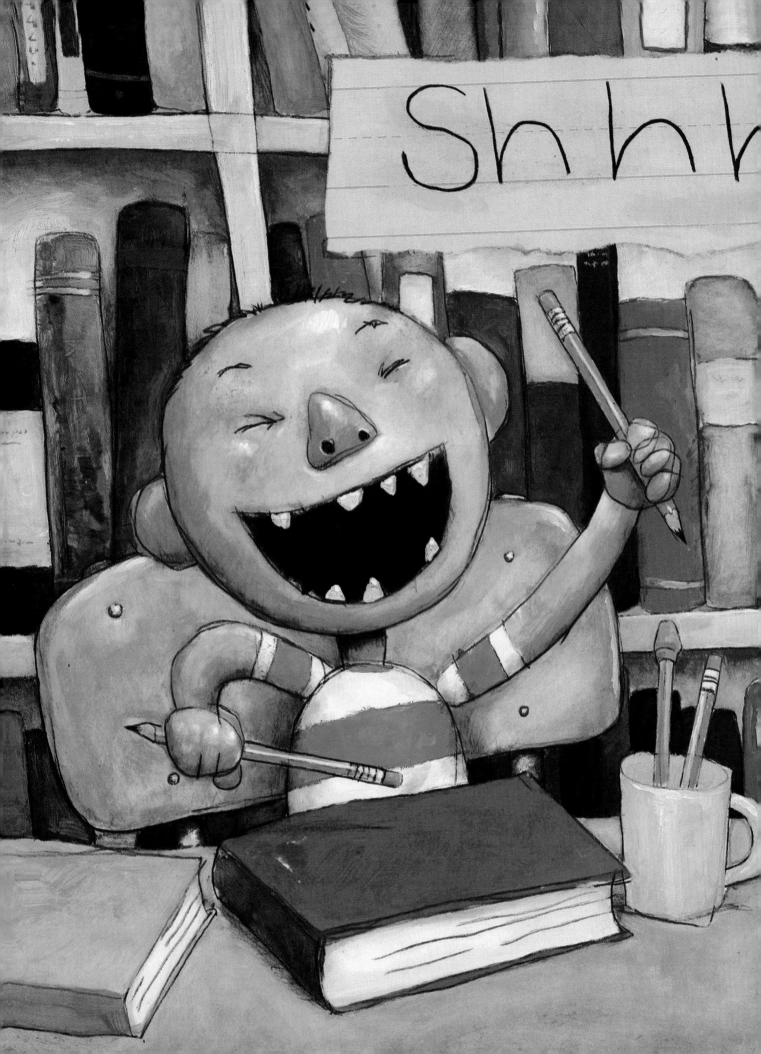

you finished?